This Special Signed Edition of

The Bone Lantern

is Limited to 100 Copies.

Angela Slatter

Angela Slatter

THIS IS COPY

THE BONE
LANTERN

THE BONE LANTERN

Angela Slatter

The Bone Lantern
Copyright Angela Slatter © 2022

Cover Art
Copyright Daniele Serra © 2022

Introduction
Copyright Marie O'Regan © 2022

This hardcover edition is published in May 2022 by Absinthe Books, an imprint of PS Publishing Ltd, by arrangement with the author. All rights reserved by the author.

The right of Angela Slatter to be identified as Author of this Work has been asserted by her in accordance with the Copyright, Designs & Patents Act 1988.

This book is a work of fiction. Names, characters, places and incidents either are products of the author's imagination or are used fictitiously. Any resemblance to actual events or locales or persons, living or dead, is entirely coincidental.

ISBN
978-1-78636-834-8
978-1-78636-833-1 (signed edition)

Design & Layout by Michael Smith
Printed and bound in England by TJ Books

Absinthe Books
PS Publishing | Grosvenor House
1 New Road Hornsea, HU18 1PG | United Kingdom

editor@pspublishing.co.uk | www.pspublishing.co.uk

INTRODUCTION

It's a delight to be able to welcome Angela Slatter to the Absinthe Books stable for its second year. I've long been a fan of her writing and have been lucky enough to commission short stories from her for three anthologies so far: *Phantoms*, *Wonderland* and *Cursed*, from Titan Books, all of which were very well received.

Angela is also the author of several novels (*Vigil, Restoration, All the Murmuring Bones*, among others) and her work has won or been shortlisted for World Fantasy Awards, British Fantasy Awards, Aurealis Awards, Ditmar Awards, Australian Shadow Awards, Locus Awards and the Dublin Literary Award.

All of the above made her an obvious choice for Absinthe Books, as far as I was concerned, and I was delighted when she agreed to write a piece for us. As you'll see from Angela's Author's Note, *The Bone Lantern* sits firmly in what she refers to as the *Sourdough* world, following the character of Selke and set just after the events of *The Tallow-Wife*. Angela weaves three stories within a story, taking you deep into the Sourdough world, and what a world it is—witches, ghouls, magic and murder, all expertly interwoven.

—Marie O'Regan
Derbyshire, June 2021

THE BONE
LANTERN

To my father, Peter, who's proud of me even though he's not really sure what I do. That makes two of us, Da.

Once Upon a Time...

It's late, drawing past midnight when she hears the *pad-pad-pad* of feet—no, paws. She's travelled long, only made camp an hour or so earlier. Now Selke thinks she should have kept on a while longer. The horse, unhitched from the wagon, but hobbled and not too far from her, whinnies nervously.

She knows him for what he is as soon as she sees him though she's unsure why.

Drawn to her fire, no doubt, by the smell of the meat that's in the between-stage: still raw, not quite cooked, but warming, warming, warming, blood running again, fat dripping, all from the action of the flames.

He's leaner than a hunting hound, skin greyer than a corpsewight—and he's alive, not like those revenants that haunt graveyards and lonely places—hair a cinder-storm of knots and dirt. Naked but for a scrap of filthy fabric around his hips. Eyes amber, and there's the promise of death in them.

He's hesitant, though, as if he hasn't quite decided which shape to take. As if there's something more pressing than his desire for food. His sort, when they wander, don't do so in the daylight, they find dark places to hole up and await the safety of night.

She wonders how long he's been awake, looks without looking at the striations in his muscles. The longer they sleep, the harder the body gets, until sometimes they don't wake at all. She's never seen one before, not in all her born days, of which there have been so very many (centuries, in fact), though she recognises him from the descriptions she's read. For all her learning, stolen and inherent, she doesn't know *how* they come to be—never found that secret in any book. Just the knowledge of *what* they are. All of which doesn't mean no one knows the secret, or no one's written it down, just that she's not yet found the right tome.

He's swaying now, just a little, as if trying to decide one way or another: man or wolf, man or wolf. She carries a knife—of course she does—but it's not in her pocket as it usually is. No, oh no, it's over there on the step of the little painted caravan she took from the Singing Vine Vineyard all those months ago (its owners apparently deceased in some scuffle on the road, and the mistress of the vineyard happy enough for her to have possession of the small home). A risk, she thinks; jumping for the weapon would be foolhardy and she always calculates her odds. So, a different tack.

"Good evening,' she says equably. 'You've travelled far, I think."

He looks at her, head tilted like he's trying to decode her meaning—translate the words. His mouth opens—*my, what big teeth you have*! Startlingly white for his overall air of grubbiness—and a growl issues forth. He clears his throat, tries again. "Yes."

The voice is rough, disused, near-forgotten.

"You're welcome to share my fire, my meal," she offers as if she hadn't seen what he is, what he might do. Says it as if this is a normal encounter, two friends well-met on the road, companions to pass the dark hours. It's spring—when it hasn't seemed to be spring for so very long, such years—and perhaps that's what's woken him, brought him forth. Perhaps he was on the cusp of sleeping forever, grown entirely petrified. *Stone wolf*, she thinks, and wishes she could examine him more closely, with tweezers and scalpel, pin his skin back, open him up—that sort, so rare! Some commentators have compared them with trolls yet established no relation. But that's unlikely to happen.

She gestures to what used to be a very fat hare, roasting on a spit. The man nods, and she casually moves to catch up the knife. There, she has it now, feels better; slices chunks off, drops them onto the tin plate she was going to use herself. She's careful as she offers it to him, but he's polite, takes it with elegant yet grimy hands, thanks her nicely. He sits, cross-legged on the grass. She doesn't take any food herself—greasy fingers will put her at a disadvantage—instead she perches on the steps of the caravan. It gives her some distance from him, possibly enough time to get up and into the cabin, lock herself in. Possibly. But she doesn't know how long it would be before he tore through the flimsy wood of the doors, then her own flimsy flesh—or maybe he'll go for the poor horse first. She cannot die, at least by normal means, but she's never been eaten entirely by a wolf and shat out— she's lost a few digits here and there, always remade by her magic clay—however, *this* might be the end of her? Or perhaps she'd reconstitute somewhere unpleasant. Despite what she's seeking, she'd still prefer to choose the means. Who's to know? And she's curious about his nature—not so much about passing through the innards of a stone wolf—always has been too curious by half, though it's led her to good and ill.

"My name is Selke," she says. "Will you tell me about yourself? Have you wandered far from home?"

He looks up from pushing food into his mouth, manners thrown aside by hunger. "Some distance, yes."

Ah. Silence for a while then.

"What are you doing here?" he asks at last. The meat is gone from his plate. How long will that keep him sated? "Where have you come from? Where are you going?"

She smiles. "Seeking, as ever."

"What?"

"Things to ease my passage, pay my way, to open doors." *See, I can be mysterious too.*

"Treasure?" A greedy sharp gleam in his eyes, and she wonders how long it's been since he hungered for anything other than flesh or sleep. She wonders what he'd do with treasure, or is this avarice a leftover from when he was all human?

"Sometimes. Some are rare things, some are simply tales to point the way."

"Tales? You collect them?"

"I find them, if they are of use." She notes he doesn't ask *What way?*

"Where do you find them?" He tilts his head, eyes narrowing.

"Sometimes from the tellers, when they remain. Sometimes from books, when I can find them. Sometimes from families and friends, those who've inherited stories, retold them." *Sometimes I've lived them.*

"Don't they change them? Those inheritors?"

She shrugs. "Mostly yes. But the core stays the same, and on occasion the embellishments make the stories more themselves, more what they're meant to be."

"It's been a long time since I heard any sort of tale."

"I can tell you one, if you like?" *Buy yourself time, Selke. How starved is he for company?* She rises, cuts him more meat from the hare, hands it over. *Sate one sort of hunger for a while.*

He takes the food, nods; a slight smile, childlike at the thought of a bedtime story.

"So," she says, and sits once more, hands clasped neatly in her lap, white hair that was once so red now bright in the light of the fire. "In a place, neither near nor far, and a time, neither now nor then..."

The Tale of a Necklace

A LONG TIME AGO, WHEN LODELLAN STILL DROWNED its witches—before the city fathers found fire to be more efficient, less likely to taint their water supply, and far less likely to allow a cunning woman to slip her chains and swim away—Gwynn watched her mother die.

Rose was one of seven to be fed to the nameless river that day (including the Prince's newest wife and *not* the first of his to be drowned, but not the last). Edryd, Gwynn's father, had reported his own wife to the authorities. All the accused were the consorts of prominent men, women who'd found themselves at the wrong end of the Church's beliefs and their husbands' spite. They'd committed—or been accused of—the various sins of practices blasphemous and unnatural, but even at sixteen Gwynn knew their greatest offences were to be infertile or disobedient, or simply no longer being *new*.

Gwynn watched as her mother was walked to the edge of the dock, wrapped in chains to which a large stone block was attached. Such things were quarried in a nearby town, transported to Lodellan especially for these moments, and when enough time had passed they were retrieved for use in the building of the great cathedral. The witch-bones were scavenged under cover of darkness by those with uses for such things. Gwynn held Rose's terrified gaze as the official executioner gave her mother a single, contemptuous shove and she tipped like a falling tree, arms tied to her sides, unable to save herself or even flail wildly. Gwynn's fingers went to the necklace at her throat, a single pendant of jet on a length of silver, pushed into her hands by Rose on the morning two weeks ago when she was arrested; a hasty inheritance. Her mother did not bob to the surface like a cork for one last glance, no. She was gone so quickly Gwynn didn't think she'd even had time or the presence of mind to take one last breath.

Edryd waited a moment, nodded, then offered his arm to Gwynn and led her back inside the city walls. From that day, Gwynn never lost the habit of walking gingerly, her steps careful and considered as a cat who'd had its paws burnt. Careful steps, even more careful words, for who knew who might be listening? It didn't make her a fearful creature, however, merely cautious.

She held her tongue even when her father was at his most irrational, was respectful and never questioned him. She did, however, learn the art of suggesting ideas in such a fashion that he thought they were his own. It was a technique that stood her in good stead as Edryd taught her the part of his craft that was most useful to him: compounding medicines and elixirs. He had some small talent for it, but the activity bored him. He'd worked his way up to become chief physician to the Prince of Lodellan, and had kept his position through much cleverness and a modicum of luck (of course, one royal death would mean the end of him, possibly herself). He realised early on that his daughter had a sense for plants and their properties that he never would, and set her to work by the time she was five.

Gwynn knew that her education came purely because she was an only child, and she was rigorous in becoming indispensable. Her wondrous potions, powders and pills not only enhanced Edryd's reputation, but had the added advantage of keeping suitors at bay— or rather, of having Edryd keep them at bay. Marriage would see his daughter taken from his control and given to that of another. Children would eat even more of her time, and then what hope might he have of getting a good day's work from her? A husband for his daughter would mean entirely too much disruption in Edryd's life.

And Gwynn was glad of her father's selfishness.

There might come a time when she thought to take a husband or wife, but she was determined it wouldn't be now, and it wouldn't be in Lodellan. She had no desire to put her liberty into the hands of another man who might as easily grow bored with her as her father had her mother; no desire to be fed to the river like so much fish bait. For that moment, she was content to learn from Edryd, from the merchants and stallholders in the markets who traded in the sorts of ingredients she needed and, less openly, from those clever enough to conceal what they truly were from the authorities, lest they find themselves taking a permanent bath.

Gwynn devoted a large amount of time to experimenting with plants and herbs, flowers and fluids in the cellar workshop of her father's home. There was a fine line, she knew, between medicine and magic—and sometimes there was no line at all. What the god-hounds called a miracle might as easily be the result of the application of a particular blend of compounds, or the consequences of the ritual that went with their creation. Might be the words spoken over the mortar and the blood dripped into it and ground together with the pestle.

She frequented darkened rooms hidden behind bookcases in certain stores, learning spells, buying hard-to-acquire additives of which her father had no knowledge. She kept two books: one of "recipes" for medicinal treatments which she was quite happy to be seen with; the other could only have been called a *grimoire*, which she took care to keep hidden.

In her rare free hours, Gwynn wandered the poorer cantons of the city. The places by the outer walls where folk huddled three families to a dwelling meant for one; slept in haylofts and barns side by side with stock, on roofs, beneath buildings, anywhere they could find. She cured fever and colds, sores and other ailments. She set bones, lanced cankers, delivered babies and, when she could do nothing else, helped the sick to their final rest. Her father did not know of these excursions.

Such kindnesses gained her no coin, but she banked favours and learned a range of skills that would have caused Edryd and most of the constabulary to frown: pickpocketing, lockpicking, how to enchant the soles of her shoes so she might approach and leave any person or location silently, and how to whisper the fabric of her dresses so she might pass by if not entirely unnoticed, then at least in a forgettable fashion. The beldams in the darkest hovels sold her witch-bones from the bottom of the river, some of which might even have belonged to her mother.

When Gwynn was nineteen, Edryd finally remarried, surprising himself by choosing a woman of his own age. Gwynn thought perhaps he truly loved Lillias; perhaps he thought she might yet bear him a son, if given enough of Gwynn's potions. She was not surprised at his choice, for she'd had a hand in it herself. Lillias had arrived in the city a year before from who-knew-where, beautiful and elegant, a maker and purveyor of cunning cosmetics. She rapidly became popular with the rich women of Lodellan, and Gwynn first encountered her in some of the less approved of locations she herself frequented. They'd recognised something in each other they both kept hidden from those around them, all those fine upright folk, and struck up a friendship. They took coffee together once a week and, after several months, Gwynn, figuring a stepmother she'd chosen was better than one she had not, introduced Lillias to her father. She'd advised how best to win his favour although soon realised the woman needed no such instruction.

Within a few months, Edryd was caught and the wedding was held, attended by the rich and important. Lillias moved from her ridiculously large house into Edryd's ridiculously even larger house in the richest quarter of the city (closest to the palace) and claimed rooms for herself on the third floor. She chose a sitting room, a study and another that she kept as a locked workshop (with excuses about servants who might pilfer her stocks of expensive ingredients) where she could make her wares, having insisted upon continuing her commerce after marriage. Edryd, loath to say *no* to an increased fortune, agreed without much of a fight. Thus the new family rubbed along nicely for some months, with no one interfering in anyone else's business.

One morning at breakfast, on one of those days when Edryd had been called out to attend upon the Prince and his fussy digestion, Lillias sipped at her tea then touched the bare spot at the base of her throat and pointed to Gwynn. "What an interesting necklace."

Gwynn's fingers flew to the jet pendant lying against her skin, always cool no matter what the weather or her own temperature. "It was my mother's."

Lillias gave a sharp nod. She had been told of Rose's fate in the days before Edryd's courting, so she might know the risk she took.

"So striking. Once, it was said, there was a woman who owned such a thing hung with twelve pendants, and in each was trapped a *daimōn*."

"Truly?" Gwynn's tone was more shocked than she'd intended and it made Lillias laugh.

"Oh, it's not such a bad thing, you know. '*Daimōn*' simply means a guiding spirit. All these churchmen speak of demons with such terror, but what do they know? They try to destroy anything that frightens them, and that is anything they don't understand, and *that* covers a lot of territory." She laughed again. "They interpret things for their own gain and purpose."

Gwynn did not argue. "What happened to the necklace?"

"The woman used a piece as and when she needed to, summoning the spirit inside. The thing was passed along, mother to daughter, some using several shards, some not a single one. But gradually it was whittled down to just a single fragment."

"How strange you should know that story and tell it."

"How strange you should choose to listen."

There was a single beat of time, a pulse of blood, then they both smiled and laughed. Lillias went on her way, heading to the markets with a servant in tow to carry the four baskets of products (two for the stalls, two for personalised deliveries to rich houses and their mistresses). And Gwynn, watching from the dining room windows, skipped immediately to Lillias' workroom as soon as she saw her stepmother disappear down the lane and turn the corner.

Though she had keys to every room in the house, Gwynn knew her stepmother had changed the lock on *this* door. Thanks to her more illicit skills, she had it open in a trice. She'd always known Lillias used herbcraft for her cosmetics, but their conversation had pricked at Gwynn's curiosity; the woman clearly knew other things as well. Gwynn might have continued to ask questions, but her natural caution stayed her tongue—words might well come back to haunt her, and so it seemed preferable to commit *this* act of intrusion.

She searched swiftly and deliberately, making sure nothing was left out of place as she passed—she'd become expert at not disturbing anything in years of ransacking her father's rooms when required. It was not long before she'd found stores of foxglove (which would stop a heart), hellebore (burning of the eyes, mouth and skin, vomiting, diarrhea, rashes, even depression depending on the dose) and nightshade (paralysis, delirium, hallucination, death), which might all be used for good purposes as well as bad. At last, in the bottom of a locked desk drawer (so easily picked!) was a small black book not much larger than the size of her hand, each page covered in a tight, tidy script.

Spells.

Spells of all sorts. Were she to copy each and every one, Gwynn would need days. Yet this might be her only chance and she would have an hour or two at best before Lillias returned. She made a decision and stuffed the book into a pocket, then ran to her own room one floor down. Gwynn kept a stock of tracing paper for when she took a copy of a botanical illustration for reference, and she used it now to gently make rubbings of three pages. The imprints came through perfectly.

Three spells, three spells were all she took. Three spells she chose (stole), three only of particular interest. There's magic in three, after all.

Then she returned to her stepmother's workroom and hid the little tome. One last glance to make sure everything was in place, and she set the lock once again. Feverish to try something new.

※

The bird was heavy, bronze, a gift from her father for some birthday or other, or perhaps as a reward for saving a rich client (a woman suddenly fertile, a man cured of chest pains, a child/heir whose breathing difficulties had disappeared). Gwynn could not quite remember and didn't particularly care. It wasn't to her taste, but her father's, so he'd assumed she would like it. It rested on the desk in her bedroom, out in the open so he might spy it should he be passing by or come in to ask some question or other. Mostly, however, it was a thing she'd ceased to notice.

Yet at that moment it was the object her gaze settled upon. She'd finished transcribing the spells into her own *grimoire* and was seized by the urge to try the first spell. It was so different from anything she'd seen or done before. Usually, Gwynn's magic was directed towards acts related to her philtres and tisanes; this was something novel, the exercise of power for its own sake, to simply see what might be possible.

She had the required dried sage, cedar and rosemary, the candles and ink. She had a sharp knife. Gwynn locked the door and closed the curtains; the fire laid in the hearth to take the cold off the day gave a dim glow. She sat at her desk and, on the uppermost sheet of blotter paper, drew the circle and star therein, and put the bronze bird in the centre. She lit five candles and placed them at each point, then sprinkled the mix of three herbs over each flame. The tiny fires changed colour from orange to green, the smoke then rising blue and smelling sweet. Gwynn used the dagger to make a short, shallow cut in the crook of her elbow—easier to hide, less likely to get infected.

She whispered the incantation from the book. Soft words dropped from her mouth as she let the blood drip down her forearm to her index finger, thence to spatter on the metal flanks. A small spark spat out from her fingertip—a shock to her flesh—and heated the cold carapace. Almost immediately, the bird gave a squawk of surprise and flapped its wings, body almost fluid for a moment, next swelling as if it would burst.

The spell was to give a semblance of life, to animate objects.

The bird, clearly terrified, flew upwards then around the room, too fast and uncontrolled. It made pitiful noises: a metallic crying, a sound of fear and incomprehension, as if to ask *Why has this been done?* At last it hit the sturdy oak door, gouging out splinters, stunning itself, and falling with a crash to the floor.

Before it could take off again, Gwynn grabbed it; she covered its eyes so it couldn't see the world into which it had been thrust. That seemed to calm the creature. Beneath her hands, Gwynn could feel it shudder, but there was no movement of breath, no thud of blood through bronze veins. It felt both hot and cold. She found a scarf in the trunk at the foot of her bed and wrapped the bird gently but firmly in the fabric. Then, deep beneath layers of clothing, she buried it. In the darkness it lay mostly quiet.

It had no soul, no mind, but it had life and was terrified. The spell had been intended to animate things like chairs and tables—as a prank or a warning—with ordinary objects the force would wear off eventually, once the haunting was done. But the bird...she had not thought it through...the bird was something different: created in the image of a *living* creature. The spark of life that had flown from Gwynn's hand had grafted itself onto the thing, sunk deep into its very molecules.

It seemed there was no way to release it from its existence.

~

"She should be pregnant by now," Edryd hissed as he and Gwynn walked the corridors of the Palace towards the Wives' Wing. (Those were the days when the Prince of Lodellan had more than one spouse and any number of independent mistresses—not a habit before or after that particular ruler.)

"How long have they been married?" asked Gwynn, who honestly could not recall. The Prince's weddings were seemingly so frequent that they all ran together. The brides' faces coalesced into a single blurred image that looked like none of them, but a little like all of them.

"Almost a year. She should have fallen by now."

"Does the Prince truly require more children?" she asked quietly, her tone studiedly neutral. At last count, if Gwynn remembered rightly, there were ten sons and seventeen daughters. "He has his heir and spares to burn."

As a child she'd played with the royal vermin (as her mother was wont to call the brats), and made no special friendships for she'd found them without exception to be unexceptional, all tarred with their father's entitlement, their mothers' beauty, but nothing else to make an impression. There were more than enough daughters to marry off for alliances, sons to send to the Church. Gwynn recalled the Prince had been an only child, cosseted, raised like a hothouse flower, his parents' fear of his death intense.

"That's not the point, Gwynn!" Edryd's low pitch did nothing to hide his irritation. Gwynn recalled that the palace walls had ears as well as hidden halls and secret chambers. Maids, chamberlains, manservants listened and reported to the Prime Minister, the Treasurer, the Prince's mother, the Prince, and most of his wives and mistresses, not to mention lesser doctors jostling to take Edryd's place should he fail. All knew that information was a currency of rare value. "The point is that the Prince cannot be seen as weak in any fashion. He has sired children before; should he cease to do so, our enemies will question why. If it appears his potency has eroded in any way there will be civil unrest as other princes from minor city-states seek to take his place. His heir is still too young to rule. Why, only a month ago there were two assassination attempts. And that Duke? The jumped up 'Swan Prince'? He'd have an army of mercenaries at the gates before you know it."

"Perhaps," said Gwynn, "our Prince should not have drowned the Duke's sister."

Edryd's lips pursed and paled. He continued, "Surely it is a failing in the woman."

"The wife."

"Either she bears a child or she will be put aside, sent to a convent, or..." Unspoken was *drowned*—the dead wife in question came from a town accepting of magic, so it had been easy enough to throw that accusation. Edryd shook his head. "But even that last action... there will still be whispers that she was set aside to hide his shame."

Correct, thought Gwynn, but did not say. Instead: "Unless one of his other wives were to become pregnant?"

"Which they have so far failed to do."

"How inconsiderate," she let slip, her mind darting back to the bronze bird. She imagined she could still feel the tremor in its metal form—no breath, though, no heartbeat, no rush of blood, merely a strange animation. She'd been back to Lillias' workroom in the days since, but had found nothing in the little grimoire that might put an end to the creature's unnatural life.

"Keep such comments to yourself," Edryd hissed. "There are others looking to take my place, and my only luck is that none of them have succeeded in helping this woman."

"Wife."

"If you can make her fertile—and you *must*, Gwynn—then my position will be assured."

Until the next one lies barren. "I will do my best, Father."

"And make no mistake: your position is bound to mine." He flicked a glance at her, a narrowing of the eyes as if he might divine any secret rebellion in her.

"Of course, Father."

At last, they reached the Wives' Wing, a series of luxurious suites for each spouse and any children they had borne—some more crowded than others. Two guardsmen waited there, purple and grey uniforms, features identical for all intents and purposes, opening the gold-flecked doors in perfect synchronicity. They might well have been carved of the same piece of wood, or clockwork soldiers.

Down the corridor, right to the very end, the last door on the left. Inside: a small chamber, richly decorated. *Wise*, thought Gwynn, *not to have children. Where would she put them?*

And there was the Wife, attired in royal amethyst, the gown's bodice tight, the skirts sweeping to the floor, the sleeves intricately pintucked and slashed, beribboned and edged in silver lace so that Gwynn could not understand how the woman did anything that required purposeful movement of arms and hands. She realised quickly that purposeful things did not concern royalty. Long black hair, deep-set black eyes, high sharp cheekbones and full red lips.

Gwynn thought how beautiful the Wife was and understood the

Prince's unwillingness to give her up, to cast her aside too hastily. She looked down at her own dress: murky mud-grey, fine fabric, but not designed to draw attention; her own mother had been lovely, but Gwynn made no effort to mimic her. Better to be a live sparrow than a dead peacock.

"My lady." Edryd gave a deep bow and Gwynn remembered, belatedly, to curtsy. When she rose it was to find the woman's dark gaze directed at her in amusement.

"Physician," she replied. "Girl."

"This is my daughter, Gwynn, and the finest apothecary Lodellan has to offer."

"Better than you?"

"*I* am a physician, my lady, no mere apothecary. I have brought her to examine you so we may discuss the next best course of treatment."

"You have been singularly unsuccessful thus far, what makes you think your progeny will accomplish anything greater?" The woman raised an arched brow. Gwynn thought she'd never seen such a thing done so elegantly. Or arrogantly.

"You have resisted—or your body has—any of the usual solutions we have found work for most women. Gwynn is here to decide the next direction to try before my *final* diagnosis is given to the Prince."

Gwynn noted that her father not only managed to shift the blame to the Wife for her own ills, but also to threaten her—and leave open the chance that fault might also be apportioned to Gwynn herself. She watched the Wife colour, draw breath in so she might yell better. Gwynn stepped forward, laid a hand on her arm. "My lady, if you will permit, I will conduct an examination. My questions may seem impolite, but all this must be done to find a solution to your problem. I will help ensure your longevity in the royal household."

Edryd drew a sharp and audible breath—such bluntness!—but Gwynn sensed that nothing else would work with this woman. There was a tense moment of silence that stretched until Gwynn thought perhaps she'd miscalculated, overstepped, but then the Wife nodded, a curt jerky movement.

"You may stay," she said, then glanced at Edryd. "And you may go."

Before her father could object, Gwynn said soothingly, "This will be convenient, Father, for I know the Prince has requested your presence this morning." The Prince had done no such thing, however Edryd's pride was saved and salved. And he was clever enough to not begin an argument with her, at least not in the presence of another.

❦

In the next few weeks, Gwynn lost sleep. She lost sleep because of her twice daily visits to the palace. She would examine the Wife, take her temperature, assess her wellness and humour, insist she undertake a series of physical exertions, then mix fresh potions based on her observations for the Wife to drink down. They did not become friends— the Wife was unfailingly aloof and Gwynn wondered why she went to such lengths to help her—but she was determined to defy the Prince and her father. Determined not to give the Prince an excuse to throw another woman to the waters, and even more determined to better her father's efforts. The care of the Wife became almost all-consuming.

And she lost sleep because, at night, all she could hear was the thud and tremble of the bronze bird. Even in the darkness of the chest, even in the soft blind wrapping of the scarf, she believed it shuddered and shook, making an insistent tiny constant noise that only she would hear. During the day, the usual sounds of the house, of living, drowned out anything else, and Gwynn ignored it as long as she could. One day, however, whether through the fugue of sleep deprivation, desperation or both, a solution seemed to present itself.

It was very late in the afternoon, most folk had transacted their business, shut up shops and stalls, and headed home for the day. Gwynn moved through the shadows of an alleyway; she'd been to this establishment before, ostensibly a perfumier in the finest part of the city, but she preferred to visit closer to closing time when there were (hopefully) fewer customers. Ingredients were to be had here, and she did indeed seek some for the treatment of the Wife, but those who knew better—by whispers and necessity—and could pay the price might also acquire something more lethal. Rohesia, in addition to being a perfumier of note, was also a talented poisoner. It was said she'd read from the greatest of poisoners' bibles, *The Compendium of Contaminants*, and could brew a toxin so virulent that it would rot the flesh from a man's bones after one sniff. It was said she could infuse a garment with a powder that would kill a person in their sleep or at a grand ball, in church or anywhere, really. It was said she could make women miscarry, men impotent, and animals a means to murder their owners. Her clientele for this particular service was small and sworn to secrecy—too many mysterious deaths of inconvenient husbands would eventually be questioned, and lead to the river.

Gwynn stepped through the doorway, scanned the single large room and found, to her satisfaction, that only the owner remained, standing behind a counter and smiling lazily at her. The air smelled exotic and lovely, and the shelves glimmered with elegantly shaped bottles filled with an entire rainbow of coloured liquids.

"Mistress Gwynn, how may I help? Something fragrant, perhaps?" Rohesia was handsome, her dress a glorious ruby silk, though her skin was pockmarked. She wore a thick layer of makeup to cover it, and for a moment Gwynn thought it sad—then decided perhaps she should not, for all women find their armour where they may.

"Nothing like that." Gwynn smiled. "I am in need of your other wares."

The woman's eyes narrowed and her smile became fragile, a little less friendly. Hesitantly, she said, "Whatever do you mean?"

"Black cohosh, red clover and chaste berry." There was no great scandal in buying *those*—in fact, she could well have bought them elsewhere—but Gwynn would mix them in a different fashion to the norm for the Wife's treatment. And their purchase gave her an excuse to come to the shop.

Rohesia relaxed visibly; she gathered three small sachets and filled them from drawers beneath the counter, not bothering to ask Gwynn for quantities. When they were almost overflowing, Rohesia put them on the benchtop. "And something else?"

"And something else."

A painted brow was raised.

"Your blackest poison and no questions."

The brow went higher still. "For a husband, perhaps?"

Gwynn made an exasperated noise. "That's a question."

Rohesia smiled coldly.

Gwynn relented. "Not a husband, no. A...mistake. To fix a mistake. Nothing that will lead to your door, I swear."

"Rohesia does not judge." The woman moved towards one of the laden shelves; she shifted coloured bottles, each one making a soft clink, until there was enough space for her to touch the wall behind. Gwynn watched Rohesia's square little hand press against what appeared to be solid stone. A scraping sound echoed, and the perfumier pushed a square panel aside—by dint of clever workmanship it slid into a niche—then reached in and withdrew a vial. The thing was lovely even in a shop of lovely things; it caught the light and shone with iridescent glory. Its mouth was sealed with a stopper and beeswax, and Gwynn detected no trace of dust—it had not been in there long, which suggested such stock moved rather quickly. Rohesia held it out to her, then rummaged in a drawer. She produced a pair of black leather gloves. "Take them and use them. Do not get the mixture on your skin, do not sniff at it. When you are done, be careful how you remove the gloves and burn them. Straight onto the fire. Do not breathe the smoke."

Gwynn nodded. She slipped a pouch of coins from her pocket and slid it onto the counter. Rohesia's fingers were quick to count the contents. She gave a nod and no change.

"I was not here," Gwynn said.

"I never saw you, Gwynn," Rohesia agreed pleasantly.

Clutching the bottle tightly, Gwynn tucked the gloves away, into the space freed up in her pocket by the exit of the coin purse, then ventured forth into the almost-dusk. She headed towards home, it wasn't so far, and forced herself to walk at a normal pace; anything else would smack of guilt, would make anyone who saw her remember despite her inconspicuous attire and spelled-silent shoes.

From somewhere up ahead, in the depths of an alleyway, she heard the rumble of masculine voices. She wanted to use that thoroughfare but did not want to risk a conversation, so Gwynn stepped into a puddle of shadows and waited; surely they'd be on their way soon enough. She had a clear view of them, the Prince's men-at-arms, she thought at first—their uniforms the proper purple and grey with silver sigils on the epaulets. But they did not move along, and so she had time to study them. Still, she mightn't have paid any more attention, might have decided to slip away via another route, but there was something about their postures (slouchy, dishonest) and, moreover, the weapons hanging at their sides. The curve of the blades was more pronounced than she was used to seeing, and the hilts and guards: the former was shaped to look like a swan's head and neck, the latter like outstretched wings. Gwynn felt a chill dance up her spine; they were clearly waiting for something or someone, and soon her patience was rewarded—or punished.

Another figure came into view: smaller, more compact, wrapped in a thick dark cloak with the hood raised, a bright flash of turquoise peeking through the folds as they approached. The men straightened, nodded, and the three of them huddled together. A discussion ensued, none of which Gwynn could hear, but she watched the newcomer hand over something she could only just identify in the dim light: a large brass key suspended from the figure's fingertips. Suspiciously like the one that Edryd had to let himself into the Prince's quarters late at night when he had a standing arrangement with the ruler to attend him before he visited one of his wives. The third then pointed towards a spot in the wall that surrounded the palace, a spot Gwynn knew was currently under demolition, where the new cathedral would sit cheek-by-jowl with the Prince's residence. Easy enough to slip through at this time of day, when guards' thoughts turned to the end of shift, homecooked meals, tavern drinks, and the warm arms of the pretty maids for sale on Half-moon Lane.

The two men marched off in determined fashion, and when they disappeared Gwynn's attention turned to the remaining figure; she fought the sense of familiarity that came the moment she'd sighted this one's swaying walk. A breeze kicked up, cold, and tore at the watcher's hood, exposing for just a moment but long enough to show a smile on Lillias' face. It wouldn't have mattered, Gwynn thought, for she'd have recognised the turquoise silk of the gown Edryd had gifted to his wife not three days ago.

She'd grown to love Lillias, and Gwynn couldn't imagine why her stepmother would commit such a betrayal. What could have motivated this foolish act? Did Lillias think no one would discover her part in this? That those men, if caught, would not spill her name as easily as the Prince's blood?

And if Gwynn revealed her stepmother's actions, then what awaited Edryd? His years of service would be forgotten in a wave of distrust—a man not in charge of his wife could not be trusted to care for the city's ruler. Lillias would suffer a traitor's death, beheaded in the great square, and Edryd perhaps beside her. What of Gwynn herself? She might have been tempted to let her father go to his doom—a small angry part of her said *A just reward for what you did to my mother*—but there was no way Gwynn could have avoided the same fate.

Gwynn swallowed hard; her palms, grown slick with sweat, let slip the vial of poison. She heard it crack and break on the cobbles, and so did Lillias who spun about to stare into the thick shadows as if she could penetrate the inky gloom. There was a moment when Gwynn thought her stepmother would approach, but then Lillias turned and ran. Gwynn could hear the hissing of the poison as it ate away the stones at her feet; quickly she danced back. A waste, such a waste, but the poor bird would have to wait. There were greater troubles afoot.

⁕

Gwynn ran. She ran like never before. Beneath the panic, the fear, all the emotions stirred by Lillias' betrayal and Gwynn's choices, was the cold certainty that she'd protect her family because doing so would protect *her*. Edryd had weathered the storm of his first wife being drowned as a witch, partially because the Prince had drowned one of his at the same time—and, after all, any man might make that mistake, but for this second dangerous wife to pose a direct threat to Lodellan's royalty? At best that would appear as stupidity (and who wanted a stupid man in charge of the Prince's health?), at worst willful bad choices, maybe even collusion.

Later, perhaps, she'd consider the inherent selfishness of this, but for the moment there was only the knowledge that she did not wish to die. Certainly not like her mother. She wondered at her stepmother's actions: the result of losing a loved one either to the nameless river or the executioner's axe? Yet Lillias was not of Lodellan and Gwynn knew of no scandal attached to her. She'd come from "away" and might easily have disguised who she truly was—there had been the vaguest of tales, a sad widowing, no children to comfort Lillias, a new start in this fresh city. Might have returned for revenge. Or, perhaps the motive was as simple as monetary—her stepmother did indeed love good gold—a contract from the ruler of one of the other principalities who eyed Lodellan's worth, her fine walls, the deep coffers beneath the city, the vaults filled to overflowing by centuries of canny, penny-pinching princes. Or more simply, the Swan Prince who'd married his sister to Lodellan's violet-eyed ruler and heard of her drowning long after it was time to do anything.

Would Lillias simply disappear this eve and never be seen again? Or remain, unsuspected, at least for a while? Did she perhaps not realise that to be connected to this family when the Prince was discovered... If the false guards succeeded and fled, if the key was not found on them there would be nothing to link Edryd and his kin to the assassination. But if the guards failed, were taken alive and gave up all they knew...

Gwynn had no trouble entering the palace. She was well-known, trusted—even her desperate speed did not raise brows. The men-at-arms merely stepped aside for her as she flew towards the Prince's chambers. When she reached the doors—banded with engraved gold, pitted with amethysts—the two men there stared. Had she been fast enough? She gasped out "Assassins" and gave thanks that the soldiers did not question her, but threw open the doors.

In the large chamber: the Prince, sitting up in bed, the Wife beside him, and in front of them, on the broad expanse of the mosaiced floor, stood the would-be slaughterers, their strange swords drawn. A scream on the lips of the Wife. Gwynn gathered her breath, shouted "Protect your Prince!" and, obedient and swift, the true men-at-arms rushed forward. They were efficient and the assassins, taken by surprise, were cut down oh-so quickly.

In the aftermath—when the blood flowed more sluggishly into the spaces between the gems and pearl-dusted fragments of the mosaic tiles, when the Wife stopped her screaming, and Gwynn got her breath back—the Prince had her stand before him.

"How did you know?" he asked. Of course he knew who she was, but her life had been beneath his notice. Edryd used her potions to treat his liege, but never drew attention to his daughter. Suddenly, there she was in the full glare of the Prince's gaze.

"I saw them in the streets, Your Highness." She swallowed—her nervousness, the shaking, were only natural. The Wife, after all, was still sobbing and trembling in the bed. "I noticed their swords. I've seen the blades of your guards since I was a child." She pointed to the bodies on the floor not so far away. "Those hilts look like swans. Perhaps I panicked, but… it seemed easier to offer an apology later than…" she glanced again at the corpses.

The Prince nodded.

Gwynn clasped her hands together; it stopped her from fidgeting with the key in her pocket. When the guards had finished their task, when they'd rushed to the Prince and the shrieking Wife, Gwynn had knelt by the dead men, her back to the room so no one might see what she did even if they were to look. Fortune had smiled, and it was on the first man she searched. Then she'd risen and rushed into the small antechamber where the door that fit the key waited. It was closed—foolish, but clearly the assassins had not expected to need to escape quickly. It was the work of a moment to lock it again. No one noticed her brief absence.

"How did they get in, Your Highness?" she asked with trepidation. "Perhaps…"

She held her breath as he turned pale; she hadn't even needed to say it aloud. She could almost see the word *witchcraft* as it leapt into his mind. Gwynn shuddered, wondering how many women would drown for this. For a brief moment she considered telling all, letting Lillias go, but there was too much of her own life that would flow away with the truth. "Your Highness, may I have leave to depart? I would seek the comfort of my family. This has been… distressing."

The Prince nodded, looked at her consideringly. "You will be sent for when required. There will be more questions to answer, but we will find the truth."

No, she thought, *you won't*. But she curtseyed, an obedient servant.

As Gwynn walked the corridors of the palace, legs weak and shaking as the adrenaline ebbed, all the thoughts of what might have been began to crowd her mind. There would be no sleep for her tonight, even if the house was silent as the grave. She considered her father and stepmother. She considered the bronze bird that still whirred in the darkness of the chest. She considered her life in Lodellan and how long she might have gained for herself.

∽

It was almost a week later when Edryd called her into his study to tell her she was to be rewarded, though the official investigation had led nowhere. She sat across from him, her eyes flicking occasionally to the cedarwood box on his desk to which she'd returned the key the night of the assassination attempt, just before sitting to dine with him and Lillias. Gwynn had spoken in a nerveless fashion of what had happened. Her stepmother had looked horrified, but not guilty, and Gwynn had to admire the steel of her.

When Edryd had rushed almost immediately to the palace, Lillias had been solicitous, offering to make a tisane so Gwynn could sleep, but the younger woman demurred. Although she did not think Lillias suspected anything beyond what Gwynn had shared, she would be cautious of taking anything from her stepmother's hand for some time. Lillias questioned her closely about what she'd seen in the alleyway, and Gwynn answered calmly that she'd seen the men walking towards the break in the wall, noticed their weapons. When she at last excused herself to go to bed, she did not think her stepmother any the wiser.

Edryd's excitement that morning was palpable, she thought she might be able to see it jumping beneath his skin. His eyes were wide, fever-bright, his fingers played with a silver letter opener. "You've done me greater honour than I ever thought possible, Gwynn."

She merely nodded; he had no idea what she'd *done*, and all she wanted was to return to the shadows where she'd lived her life. In hindsight, perhaps what she should have done in the alleyway that afternoon was to simply walk out the gates of the city and not look back, never return. Calm and unpanicked, she thought that would have been the better solution indeed, to let everything and everyone one fall as they might.

"But this...*this*!" Edryd was beside himself and she wondered how much gold the Prince had promised to part with. "Marriage!"

"What?" It came out so sharply, but he didn't notice.

"Marriage. To be the Prince's newest wife." His hands levitated; he might almost have been throwing rice at a wedding, or praying.

"Father, perhaps I misheard..."

He clicked his tongue, irked. "The Prince wishes to marry you. You saved his life. What better helpmeet might he have? Closer to him than ever I could get! And you're young enough to bear children."

Gwynn wanted to scream. She wanted to overturn his desk, yell in his face, let him know what a stupid old man he was, just another in a long line of stupid, selfish old men who poisoned the world. If she could, she'd take the silver letter opener to his skin, his chest, pluck out his heart and feed it to the stray dogs who roamed the streets. If she could, she'd hold his head under the water in the bathtub or one of the city's fountains, or the river where her mother was drowned all those years ago.

Gwynn dearly wanted to scream.

But she did not.

She pressed down on the helpless rage. She nodded and swallowed. *Hush*, she said to the tempest inside. *Hush*, as her mother said to her when the men came to the house and dragged Rose away. *Hush*, Gwynn crooned, all the while smiling as if she might be a blushing bride.

Hush.

❧

In the centre of her room, door carefully locked, Gwynn sat cross-legged in the centre of a pentacle carved into the floor (she would roll a rug over it when she was done) and topped with salt for extra strength, candles burning at each point of the star. In one hand she held a dove (its body juddered like the bronze bird), and in the other her sharp knife, which she pulled across the dove's throat with only the slightest hesitation. The desperate cooing was cut off. Gwynn swallowed. The blood welled, thick and dark. She tightened her fist around the dying creature, helped the flow, watched the droplets fall onto the necklace lying in the bottom of the copper bowl in front of her. Slow smears formed across the surface of the single piece of jet.

"Come to me, Mother, come to me now." She shifted a little to ease the ache in her hips. She spoke the words of the second stolen spell from Lillias' book. It was an incantation to summon old love, and Gwynn had only ever had one true love. But she was no fool. The lesson of the bird had been engraved on her heart; she took precautions, as one must when dealing with the dead.

A wind that had no source blew, making the candle flames dip and sway, but they remained alight. A shape moved in the gloom, something pale and torn, something that seemed to step through a doorway slashed in the dark. Gwynn smelled decay, mildew, heard water drip onto the bare floor beyond the light.

"Mother?" Her own voice sounded strange, tentative. Silence, then a harsh rattle as if the lungs that drew in breath had been deprived of it for an age. Then the gurgle, the pop of bubbles, air long and miserly held to no effect. "Mother?"

Rose flew at her from the shadows, hands clawed, teeth sharp, holes in her dress and her skin, black hair dull and twisted thick as seaweed ropes. Gwynn flinched but Rose bounced away as if she'd encountered an invisible barrier. Gwynn threw an anxious glance at the circle; as long as she stayed inside it, she was safe. Rose, staggered, threw herself forward again, bounced away once more. She dropped to her knees, half-crawled until her raised hands encountered the wall surrounding Gwynn, then she shuffled around and around, trying to find a crack, a way to the flesh within.

Gwynn watched; her breathing slowed, her heartbeat returned to normal. What had she pulled back? Where had her restless mother been, or this part of her at least? Rose looked starved. *Ghoul*, Gwynn thought, then spoke aloud: "Ghoul."

Her mother stopped, found herself named. A gleam of cunning stole into her eyes; she formed words, assayed the sounds: "Gwynn. My Guinmarie. My little girl."

Her hands became beseeching, made shapes in the air, showing how she would caress her daughter if only she could *touch* her. Gwynn was heartbroken but not foolish. The ghoul was a cannibal—she'd heard enough whispers over the years of disturbed graves and dispersed bones; sometimes they rose in the graveyard of their own accord—and no matter what Gwynn had meant to her in life, Rose was ruled by her hunger in death.

"Mother, the necklace." She gestured to the blood-smeared jewellery in the bottom of the bowl. Rose's gaze followed the direction of the slender fingers, lit upon the jet. "Mother, how do I free what's inside?"

Rose's look was blank. "What's inside?"

Gwynn doubted, now, how much of her mother truly remained. "The *daimōn*, Mother, within the stone. How do I release it?"

"Within the stone?" Rose repeated slowly, then laughed a ragged sound, limned by spite. "If I had a *daimōn* to do my bidding, *daughter*, don't you think I would have used it to cheat the river, left you all behind?"

Gwynn opened her mouth, closed it again. If Rose had been any kind of a witch, she'd have escaped. If she'd known of the secret in that single stone, she'd never have handed it to Gwynn, would have left her daughter and husband to their fate. But she was only a woman, all she could do was drown—and Edryd had known that, known she had no greater power, the same way all those husbands knew they sent helpless women to the water. *This*, Gwynn told herself, *was not her mother*. But it *was* a monster in Rose's body, and could access her memories. Gwynn just had to convince it to do so. "Where did it come from? The necklace?"

"My grandmother," said the ghoul-mother, as if they were reminiscing on a sunny day. "She told me..."

"Yes?" Gwynn knew she sounded too anxious. The creature smiled, sly. Gwynn changed tack. "Where have you been, Mother?"

Rose's teeth showed, blackened and broken in places. "Beneath the water, my sweet, my pearl, with the other unwanted, wicked dead. In the darkness between the beats of a heart. Now you summon me, up into the light all these years later." She laughed, gesturing to the blackness around them. "Why did you bring me here?"

"Would you feed, Mother? On Father?" In spite of everything Edryd had done, Gwynn felt the betrayal pull in her stomach like a lost child.

Rose's eyes narrowed, avid, greedy. "Husband? Where is he? Oh yes, I would feast on his flesh, chew on him like a dog." She clapped her hands. "Where is he, daughter-mine? Tell me where to find my meal!"

Gwynn shook her head.

Rose smacked her lips. "What's your price, child?"

"The necklace. What did your grandmother say?"

"Shall I whisper it to you? Lean close for my throat is dry and my voice fails."

Gwynn leaned forward, near enough to feel her mother's fetid breath on her cheek. Rose ran a crooked finger down the invisible wall, as if caressing. "She said my blood would aid me."

The ghoul-mother lunged once more, without much hope, and was again repelled. The creature screamed in frustration. "Where is he?"

Gwynn, hand shaking, raised the copper jug that sat beside the bowl. She raised it high, tilted it. "Go back to sleep, Mother."

"Traitor child!"

Water poured from the lip of the jug, clean and bright. It washed the blood from the stone and Rose faded away, as if scrubbed out of existence by a wet rag. The sound of her enraged shrieks stayed in Gwynn's ears long after she'd opened the windows, let the moonlight in, cleared away the evidence of what she had done, and rolled the carpet back over the marks on the floor. Tempting though it was, feeding Edryd to her mother felt like a step too far, no matter what he'd done. That night, she slept like the dead, and not even the gentle whir and thud of the bronze bird disturbed her rest.

※

In the days that followed Gwynn felt sure Lillias would *know*; that the woman would sense there was something about her, discern a reflection of Rose's image in her eyes, realise that something had been done, shifted, changed. That Lillias would smell the whiff of magic on Gwynn's skin, hear the whisper of the name her mother gave her, *Guinmarie*, which her father had never used.

But nothing happened.

Or rather, nothing except preparations for her wedding; those went on without Gwynn's minimal participation. She smiled at Lillias as the woman pointed out the fabrics, hairstyles, jewellery and scents the Prince's people paraded before them (wedding organisers had prospered under his rule). Her stepmother instructed her on the finer

THE BONE LANTERN

points of wedding night seductions; Gwynn agreed and discussed, pretended to care. She smiled at her father whenever he brought up how clever she'd been in saving the Prince, as if it were a calculated act to bring them all to this happy juncture. As if she'd wanted *this*. For all intents and purposes she was a willing bride.

⁕

The jewellery hung heavily upon her, dragged at the wrists, pulled on her neck like a gilded millstone. Rings made her nimble fingers lumpen and slow. Gwynn raised her hand to the only thing to bring comfort: Rose's necklace. It was at odds with the rest of her attire, neither rich nor showy, but she had refused to take it off and Lillias had let the matter lie.

The ceremony had taken place out in the open, in the square where the magnificent cathedral was still being built. The archbishop officiated, the rows of other wives lined the makeshift aisle of red carpet, all eyeing her; yet only the Wife appeared hostile when Gwynn glanced at her through the thick white lace veil. *Strange*, she thought.

There had been a feast in the palace's great hall, yet such a small gathering—the nuptials so quickly arranged that few nobles had been able (or willing) to make the journey. Besides, the Prince's weddings had become so frequent that no one felt they were missing anything— there would be another, after all. Thus, his speech about how Gwynn had saved him and that this was the best reward he could think of, was to those who already knew. Some perhaps thought but would never say that such a reward was barely distinguishable from a punishment.

Now, as Gwynn made her way along the corridors of her new home, the bells on the hem of her gown sounded, sad and reluctant. The garment wrapped around her like a silken restraint, constricting, constraining. She'd been wed—barely listened to the words spoken, managed "Volo" before retreating to her own thoughts—she was now a *wife*. She trod the path to the bridal chamber alone; the guards posted in their usual positions barely looking at her. The Prince waited.

As she passed a small alcove, Gwynn heard her name called. She stopped, looked to the left. A curtain had been pulled aside and the Wife waited there, swaying and pushing out a breath fetid with wine.

"Bitch," she said. "Cunning little whore. All this to take my place."

Gwynn laughed in astonishment, a powerful snort. "Fool," she spat. "Why would I *want* this?"

"Power." Fingers pointed. "Advancement."

"Only an idiot would advance themselves closer to the river."

The Wife glared, clutched at her own belly as if in pain. "Did you poison me? Did you make *this* worse so I might not have children? So I might be entirely put aside?"

Gwynn stared, shook her head. "Fool," she said again. "Absolute and utter fool."

And she turned away, continued her journey. Not so long since her hectic run to warn this man, to save him. Such a short time, and now so changed. When she at last arrived at the Prince's chambers, the men-at-arms opened the doors without looking at her. Just like that, she realised, her face had joined that blurred tapestry of all the wives who'd gone before her. Gwynn lifted her chin, drew in a deep breath, and stepped over the threshold with her head held high.

※

Stripped of his finery her husband looked smaller. He wore a simple white robe and his blond hair was loose and straight. The smile he gave his new bride was gentle, and if she'd not known better she might have thought him a fine enough husband to have. He didn't look like a bad man—but then, how many did?—but he looked just like others of his ilk. He sat on the edge of the bed, settled among the cushions and silks, and gestured for her to approach.

Gwynn let her eyes roam around the room. She had not really taken it in, the night of the assassination. Luxurious, extravagant, when so many had so little. She should not judge for she'd benefited from her association with this royal house; some might regard her current situation as a bounty, an *honour*. She could, she thought, stay for a while. See what influence she might amass, how much she might turn his mind from witchcraft and drownings. But Gwynn knew it more likely that she would simply hasten her own demise. Or, she considered, she could do what Lillias had failed to accomplish.

She shook her head. "Please know that I did not want this marriage, but I mean you no harm."

The Prince watched, perplexed. When Gwynn produced the dagger from her sleeve, his perplexity turned to fear. He scrambled back on the bed as if she might lunge at him; his expression said he had not expected this. Gwynn laughed and turned the blade on herself, this time drawing the sharp edge across her palm, a thin short line. Blood welled and she wiped it on the jet pendant at her throat. Some dripped down onto the front of her wedding gown. She whispered the words of the third spell she'd stolen—a spell for coming forth.

For a few moments nothing happened. Gwynn thought herself lost, her gamble, her guess, her hope all for nothing. The Prince's mouth opened to raise the alarm, his face darkening. She would be beneath the surface of the river before dawn.

The sound of thunder startled them both and a great wind tore through the suite, scattering vases and cushions, books and trays and glasses, clothing and bedding. Lightning split the outer wall, leaving a scorch mark on the mosaic and a gap through which the blue-black of night could be seen. The Prince was pushed back by the blast, tumbling across the silken bedspread; only Gwynn stood firm in the eye of the storm as the jet dropped from its silver chain and hit the floor. The doors shuddered as the guards tried to enter a room sealed by magic.

The *daimōn* was huge, shining like obsidian, with the eyes of a crow. It unfolded itself, body neither male nor female, until its head scraped at the ceiling. A voice rumbled up, seeming to come from the ground, thrumming through Gwynn's every extremity like the heartbeat of the earth itself.

"What is your bidding?" It threw a glance at the Prince, who cowered against the wall. "Has this one offended?"

"No!" Gwynn said. "No. Just take me from this place. Take me far away." She looked at her husband. "Promise no one will look for me."

Wordlessly wide-eyed the Prince nodded. Gwynn could see in his expression the question *Why would I hunt down a wife who commands such a creature?*

The *daimōn* gathered her up and they flew out the chasm in the wall. Swooping above the roofs of Lodellan, the *daimōn* barely visible against the night sky, the trailing draperies of Gwynn's wedding gown glinting like spider-silk in the moonlight.

Whispers of Gwynn circled for a few months. Gossip in the marketplaces had the royal groom murdering his new bride when he found her not to be a virgin. That was succeeded by the tale that she had run off with a guardsman, although no one could say who it might have been as none were missing. Those who noted the schism in the palace wall did not listen to any rumour, only prayed she would never return. Edryd and Lillias were sent forth from the city in shame—the physician's years of service gained him his life; whatever happened to them is as much a mystery as Gwynn's fate. Eventually, she faded from daily memory, only to be resurrected when stories needed to be told, lessons needed to be taught, of wives who did not conform, of girls who carried their mother's tainted blood in their veins.

THE BONE LANTERN

The Prince of Lodellan took no more brides from that day on. And the Wife? She bore a son not twelve months later.

⁂

"Such a tale, such a lie," sneers the man, the light of the flames catching in his eyes, the shadows thrown by his features turn his expression malign. Then he concedes: "Though you tell it well."

Selke lifts a brow, hesitates. Normally she'd not be at all bothered about being called a liar, but for some reason this irks her.

She imagines, perhaps, that her own son might have looked like this if he'd lived. That they might have spent such a night telling tales, travelling. Or perhaps in a fine house in Lodellan with the boy's father, the Archbishop Narcissus Marsh, who'd managed to die twice (but only once at Selke's hand). Perhaps, if their boy had survived, Selke would have had a normal span, lived and died in that city, creating the things she wished and willed. Perhaps there'd have been other children to keep that first one company, and cause a scandal for the Archbishop to father more offspring than the ruler of Lodellan.

But that boy had died.

And Narcissus had grieved so deeply he'd lost his mind, demanded she bring the child back to life. She'd refused, and run, yet so many years later she'd done that very thing—or something very like it—to her once-beloved. Long life and loneliness had changed her mind; their few strange years together had been...something.

And Selke herself has attained such a great age. Through magic she'd found a means to prolong her own existence; perhaps for too long. She now doubted that she could die, and so death had become something she desperately sought.

She smiles, rises and goes into the wagon. The sounds of rummaging fall from the doorway, then she reappears, a blue velvet sack in her grip. She reaches inside and pulls out a silk-wrapped bundle. She unfurls it to show a small bronze bird lying in her hand. They both stare at it in silence, then the thing twitches. Its thin legs and claws spasm, the beak opens, closes. Selke rewraps it quickly, buries it deep in the bag, then returns the bundle to the caravan.

When she sits back down, she brings two apples, throws one to the man. She opens her mouth, but he interrupts.

"Tell me another story. Please." He begins to crunch on the red shiny fruit with those sharp white teeth. Childlike, he adds, "Please" around half-chewed apple.

Selke looks out into the night, judging its shades of darkness, calculating how many hours until sunrise. The knife feels heavy in her pocket, the weight comforting. "Before there was a beginning..."

The Tale of a Harp

You'll not have heard the name, for the place was destroyed so long ago that few remember enough to even tell tales of its living and its ending. There was a castle that clung to a cliff, and at the mountain's feet huddled a town—or perhaps it was big enough to be considered a city, but that's neither here nor there. There were paths between the two: one wound its way up the cliff-face, open to air and sun, the summer path. Another, a tunnel cut into the rock for wet weather or winter transport of goods and such, and for the things the dukes preferred kept secret from their people. Others still honeycombed the mountainside, but unknown to most of the inhabitants of either town or the castle, and they do not concern us besides.

Once upon a time, some earlier duke had loved art and fine things so very much that he'd invited—indeed lured—such artisans as he could to live in the town. Jewel-smiths and metal-smiths, armourers, weavers of silks and tapestries, painters and mosaic-makers, crafters of musical instruments and beautiful furniture. He promised them a fine living and so they came, and, in general, they were not disappointed. The burg's reputation grew and grew, and subsequent dukes, if not entirely as enamoured of art as their predecessor, were at least as enamoured of the gold it brought to their coffers in the forms of taxes and tithes. Children learned the craft from their parents, took over businesses, passed the knowledge onto their own offspring, and so it went for generations.

The castle was an ugly thing, built originally with naught but defence in mind. Inside was a different matter: each room a cave of wonders, a treasure house of the finest things the townsfolk produced (and some items smuggled from elsewhere so as not to cause his people to feel jealous). Ceilings studded with gems so they appeared as the night sky when candlelight danced across them, thick carpet underfoot only in those places not embellished by mosaic portraits of previous dukes and their families, furnishings so lovely guests were reluctant to sit upon the chairs and lounges lest they somehow besmirch the things by their mere presence. There were paintings and tapestries on the walls, suits of armour fit only for admiring, statues in corridors and alcoves, musical instruments as lovely as the dawn.

The town, however, was picturesque and the houses a mix of wood and stone covered in vines and creepers—the inhabitants fought the incursion of the foliage indoors, but left the exteriors to be greened over by a determined forest. Flowers bloomed and ran riot across thatched rooftops, crept from the cracks in plaster; tree branches led from the upper window of one house to that of another, a handy bridge for lovers or children. The streets and alleys—required as thoroughfares for goods and carts, people and animals—were kept brightly clean, weeds swiftly yanked from any cracks between the cobbles and disposed of in fireplaces so they'd never cause more offence.

Beyond the houses came the workshops, lower down the slope and separated from the homes by a wide street—a firebreak if truth be told. It was not unheard of for the metal-smiths and glass-blowers and blacksmiths to be the source of an occasional conflagration. Along the outer boundary curved the cemetery, where the dead might be buried without poisoning the water supply or being unearthed in heavy rains that might wash them through the town, but rather down the hillside with no one the wiser for a while at least. Beside it was a small church and tiny manse inhabited by a single god-hound, relatively new to the position and overly enthusiastic.

So many workshops, but only one was of concern: the dim room where Wilm the Harp Maker once plied his trade, and where one of his daughters now found herself stuck.

She'd never thought to inherit her father's mantle so soon. In the cluttered space Alix sat, not moving, but staring at the ceiling where hung the bodies of seven dital harps, in various stages of development. They'd all spent time in the tanks—one filled with manure, the other with a mix of blood and water and wine. Their forms glowed in the lamplight. These weren't the usual sort, not large but rather something that could sit easily in a lap, and could sound as much like a lute as a harp. And they weren't so much made as grown; musical homunculi. A modicum of magic was poured over them to make them the finest they could be. Alix had helped her father tend these from the very beginning—as she had others since she was small, just barely big enough to reach the benchtops. The smell might have been overpowering to others, but Alix breathed in deeply. It was the scent of her father. It would permeate her own skin; now that *this* was hers and he had no further need of the place.

The sound of his singing would no longer lift the darkness from this little sanctuary as he taught his eldest daughter his craft. She imagined Wilm now sang only for the dead.

She looked down at the unfinished harp before her, lying in its cradle, where it had sat since Wilm first fell ill. He'd felt faint, he told her when he still had breath, but he was careful to set the thing gently in its resting place. They could not afford for the instrument to be smashed. It waited patiently now for the final attentions—and its finishing was essential if Alix planned to pay the bills her father had left behind, and to feed herself and her sister. The Duke's patience would not last much longer; if Alix could not keep the business going, the girls would be out of their home very soon. Only the fact that this particular harp was earmarked for the Duke himself had kept them safe the past few months of Wilm's sickening and dying.

Alix reached out; she hesitated, and her hands shook. She steadied them with an effort of will and blinked away tears. Tears were wasted on the dead, but the living would weep if those around them forgot to look after their own; if they lost themselves in mourning then those who relied on them would soon be lost too. There was Ide; Wilm had entrusted Alix with the care of her twin and it was an obligation she would honour, no matter how she chafed against the life.

Her fingers, long and slender, closed about the neck of the small harp. The purchase of the required materials had incurred a much larger debt than Wilm would usually have taken on. Ebony frets, bejewelled tuning pins, the wood was imported—the local trees would not render up anything sufficiently fine for the Duke—and the mother-of-pearl inlays had been wrested from the ocean, so very far away, carried in the pack of an itinerant tinker who passed through the town perhaps once a year.

Alix had never seen the sea—could not even dream of it because it was beyond her imagining and experience—but sometimes at night she was sure she heard something that might be the crash of waves. Even Wilm's tales of it, the place where he'd met and wooed her mother, were insufficient. Alix knew it only as an absence and a longing. Her parents had married while Wilm travelled to finish his apprenticeship, finding Meri in a coastal village on his long road. Wedded to the town of his birth, sworn to return there and take up his father's business, Wilm brought his bride with him, as was the way of things. Separated from her element, in the mountains, the forest,

THE BONE LANTERN

Meri grew weak and pale. She faded. Her lungs missed the salty air so much that she gave up on life not long after delivering her daughters. Wilm regretted it, felt guilty for it, and he tried to make up for the lack. He worked hard to put food on the table, made sure Alix learned his craft so she would not have to rely on anyone else for a living, and he always made time to play with them, so they would not forget they were, after all, children. Wilm had not intended, however, to die so soon, for the fever from who-knew-where to carry him off just after the girls had turned eighteen.

Beneath her fingers, the instrument felt warm, welcoming, and that encouraged her. All that remained to do was to set the inlays, the frets, the bridge, to string the creation, and then to "spell" it; to enchant the thing so it made the purest sounds it possibly could. She caressed the body and tested the strength of the neck—there was no reason to think her father's work had been less than perfect. As she laid out the tools she would use, she began, unconsciously, to hum then to sing.

It might have signalled a restoration of normality; something Alix was desperate to welcome.

※

Shall we consider the Duke himself?

He overlooked the town from his castle, through the windows of the reception hall, finely blown and thin, expensively made and beautifully engraved by some long-gone glassworker. They did not keep the room especially warm, but they separated him from air that might have been through the lungs of those who lived below.

His father had been an older style of ruler, had loved his people and visited them regularly, ensured they fared well, took care of those who fell ill and for a time could not work. He delighted in entering workshops, learning new and clever hobbies, pretending he was somehow like them. But Pol was not such a man, no—he had inherited different ideas, these from his mother. She was a princess from somewhere important, embarrassed by her espousal to a mere duke (she was well past marriageable age when she finally accepted him, was relieved and proud to produce two children soon after), and she had loathed her husband's habits, his joy in his *peasants*.

She herself had no desire to rule, so she was patient. When Pol was old enough to take the reins of the little dukedom, her husband suddenly and sadly died; one of those thin windows not properly latched, a puddle of water in the path the old Duke trod every morning as he paced the hall. A long drop, a sharp stop, and not a bone left intact in his portly corpse. They'd fair had to scoop him into a box to bring him home for burial in the family crypt.

His mother had always called Pol the "swan prince" though he had no right to such a title. Yet she'd insisted, had brought with her a family crest featuring a cygnet wearing a golden chain and crown. Her husband so liked the look of it, he'd had special swords made for his personal bodyguards, the hilts shaped like a swan's neck and head, the cross-guard in the form of its outstretched wings.

One of Pol's first acts as Duke was to send his younger sister—her name is as lost as that of the place from which she came—off to marry the Prince of Lodellan. Perhaps it had seemed a fine alliance, and Pol conveniently ignored the fact that his new brother-in-law had already drowned several of his wives for magic-related sins. Unfortunately for his sister, she produced no children and after less than two years of wedded bliss, she met a watery end. After that, the Prince married again and again and again, and it would be fair to assume he never thought of his swan princess again.

Though he never spoke of it to anyone, not even his mother, the Duke never forgot or forgave the slight. It had long been his habit to sit in his hall, listening to airs played by the musicians he'd imported from far and wide. The music, he said, soothed his mind, gave him clarity, and enabled him to see solutions that might not have otherwise presented themselves.

Indeed, a love of music was the sole trait he shared with his father, and in his middle years he had determined at last to learn to play himself. He especially loved the sound of the dital harps produced by Wilm. He was impatient for Alix to finish her work. He could not imagine that his ardent adoration would not translate into talent.

And so, he waited.

⁓

As Alix returned home at the end of the day, she passed Old Anese.

The woman sat, as was her wont, in the market square, on the wide stone edge of the fountain. Whisper had it that she'd been the wife of one of the previous dukes—set aside for any number of reasons—but she never confirmed or denied it. Yet this was a town that tolerated witches—unlike others that might be mentioned and how else could one explain the beauty of the artworks produced?—and so she was in no danger of either drowning or burning. No one knew her true age, though she was wrinkled as a raisin, and lived in a small cottage that bordered the graveyard. Said cottage was better than it should have been for a supposedly penniless crone. Her smile was warm, though, and her eyes bright, and Alix had never felt any sense of threat from her. Wilm had always been polite to the beldam and his daughters followed suit.

"Good e'en, Alix," she said.

"Have you had a good day, Mistress Anese?" Alix made a point of stopping to chat, not walking by as if she had too much else to do. "What can you tell me that I did not know before?"

The old woman smiled. "The city of Lodellan? Where the Prince has so many wives he puts value on none?"

Alix nodded. *The place where he drowns witch-wives at his*

convenience, she thought but did not say. She recalled when the Duke's sister left on her bridal procession. Wilm had made a harp to be taken on that journey, a gift for someone or other, or to show what beautiful things could be made in a town that tolerated magic, yet that magic was one of the reasons the girl was so easy to condemn. Alix had wondered, on occasion, what happened to it.

"He thought to take yet another, but this one—finally!—was a true witch!" Anese cackled, all delight at the Prince's well-deserved misfortune.

"Did she kill him at last?"

Old Anese spat in disgust. *No.*

"She summoned a *daimōn* to get her hence, out of that city and away from that husband." She laughed again, such a belly laugh that she farted almost as loudly.

"And the Prince?"

"Has repudiated all his wives but the oldest, the mother of the largest number of his children. Sworn he'll take no more."

"And the other wives?" Alix felt a tightening in her gut.

"To convents, the lot. Even the one they believed barren—who is now fit to burst soon with child—all to spend the rest of their lives in peaceful contemplation."

"No doubt a happy relief to them all." Alix let her breath out; she wondered at how that kept wife regarded her *luck*. "A better fate than so many of their sisters."

"Certainly. The battle abbeys will take some, I suspect—those with no wish to contemplate the nature of someone else's god. Those inclined to roam will find a better life there."

"Where do you think she went? That true witch?"

Anese shrugged. "As far away as possible if she's got a lick of sense." She stretched. "Best get home to that sister of yours before she frets. Little hen."

Alix grinned. "Can I bring you a meal this evening?"

The old woman shook her stick at Alix to shoo her. "Get away with you. The day I can't cook my own dinner is the day they put me in the ground."

"Good night, Mistress Anese."

"Good night, Alix."

❧

"Thank you, sister." Alix leaned back and rubbed her belly, which was not noticeably larger than before she sat down to the repast her sister had prepared. She did not put on weight, though her twin fought to keep from growing round. Perhaps it was the height difference: as tall and willowy as Alix was, Ide was short. Perfectly formed, their faces identical—dark eyes, dark hair, skin so pale as if the moon lived beneath it—but their bodies were two extremes. Ide, in her grumpier moments, claimed it was Alix's greed, to take all the height and leave her with so little. Alix let her sister have these moments; she would agree *Yes, I am a glutton*. And eventually Ide would calm down and laugh.

"I made too much," said Ide. "I forgot Father would not be with you. Even after all these weeks..."

Ide tended the home while her sister and father spent their days in the workshop. The cottage was small: two bedrooms, a bathroom, a kitchen and sitting room, all kept neat and tidy; the rugs and cushions and hangings bright splashes of colour to cheer the space. She taught music to the children whose parents would afford such indulgence, and thus brought in the small income the girls had been living on after Wilm sickened and died.

"The workshop is so quiet," said Alix, rising to clear the plates. "We will feel like this for some while, Ide."

"We will feel like this forever, sister." Ide looked at the tablecloth that had been embroidered by their mother as she waited for them to arrive. Fish and whales, their father had said, pointing to each image, and the mermaids with their long tails entwined each with each, long hair streaming behind them as they swam forever around the fabric. The girls had no actual memories of their mother, only their father's tales of her: what she said and did, how she looked ("Look in the mirror, my poppets."), what she'd owned and left behind. Things they conserved like relics, as if through touch they might connect to Meri, as if they might know her by the cloth, the pair of pearl earrings, the dresses in the chest, most of which were crumbling, crumbling, crumbling with every passing hour, yet must be kept.

"Yes," sighed Alix. *Or you'll make a point of not forgetting and of not allowing me to do so either.* The thought surprised her, hurt her a little; she did not know from whence it had come, but couldn't deny the truth of it. She would be here forever, in this house with her sister forever, in the workshop forever, eking and living, the skin of her hands splitting and drying until they looked like they belonged to a hag like Anese, and her face following sooner than it should. Old, old, old before her time and all her chances for anything else gone. Before she could dredge another reply from herself, something to soothe her sister, Ide spoke again.

"When will the Duke's harp be ready?"

Alix raised a brow. "When it is ready."

Ide hurried on, recognising her sister's prickly disposition on the rise. "I ask not to nag, but simply because he sent his steward today to see if I would provide lessons when it was ready."

Alix blinked. She'd not thought of that. Had assumed Duke Pol would import some music master from elsewhere to turn him into a virtuoso, or have one of his pet musicians do it. Her own brief conversations with the steward he'd sent twice a week since Wilm's death had been a struggle for her not to snap and snarl. If she was honest, it was also part of the reason she'd been slow to re-start the work.

"He will pay," Ide added.

"Of course, he will." Alix looked at her sister from the sink. "Do you want to do this? He's not a pleasant man, he is not kind like the old Duke. Father did not take to him—and you know Father liked *everyone*—he was polite merely because our future depended on Pol's patronage, him allowing us to remain here and ply our trade. But he is not kind, Ide."

"He doesn't need to be kind in order to learn. *I* need to be kind in order to teach."

Alix watched as her sister's expression set: the lips just-so, the chin slightly jutted, the eyes downcast. Ide would do what Ide would do. So Alix nodded and said no more than, "By the end of the week, the harp will be complete."

༄

In the reception hall, Alix waited.

She stared at the wall above the liege-chair, a work of art by some long-dead craftsman—the Duke of the time on a cloud, holding a harp while he painted, mouth open to sing (she assumed), and around him gathered wispy muses in the form of pretty, pale girls. It was studded with diamonds, pearls and rubies and she imagined how it would appear in the evenings by the flickering light of torches.

Alix had been there before, but not for many years, not since she was small and had accompanied Wilm. Funny how she hadn't remembered the ceiling, for surely she was more wide-eyed and curious then? Or, perhaps, *then* she was simply fascinated by her father, who spoke gently and respectfully to the old Duke, who'd smiled and laughed as if Wilm was his equal while Pol, the Swan Prince, glowered in the background, his stick-thin mother hovering at his shoulder, pouring whispers into his ear. Alix had never known what made him so angry, but even back then his rage had been an almost palpable thing.

Everything and everyone had seemed so big in those days. Now, a head taller than most of the men in the town, Alix couldn't help but think how small everything was, even here. How the gilt and shine, the gems and gold leaf and all the fine things were so...wasted. Who ever saw it apart from Pol and his mother, the steward and castle servants, the occasional blue-blooded visitor from away? Everything shone, she was sure, only when someone looked at it; she wondered at the cost of any one of these beautiful things. Yet the Duke had threatened them with eviction if their tithes were not paid, the death duty for Wilm, when he himself had such excess. Her fingers itched as she imagined how long she and Ide might be able to live off the proceeds of just one ruby, just one pearl. How far she might be able to travel on the proceeds of one tiny, tiny theft.

Alix shuffled awkwardly. Thoughts of running away had been in her mind before Wilm's death, though she'd admit it to no one. She moved closer to the row of tall arched windows that gave a view out onto the valley, admired the workmanship of the etching (flowers and fruit), and thought briefly what a strange blue the sky was. Then she realised it was the reflection of her blue velvet dress; at Ide's insistence she'd exchanged her usual long dark calico skirt and rough shirt (work clothes stained with dye, and the like) for a full-length gown that had belonged to their mother. It mostly fit. Ide, with great effort, had pulled a brush through her sister's thick black locks, so Alix was as close to presentable as she was likely to get. When Ide had suggested some makeup, perhaps, Alix had given her such a look as to silence her sister.

In Alix's arms lay the silk-wrapped bundle she had carried oh-so-carefully up the mountain path, fearful of slipping and dropping, of scratching or injuring her charge. Though she'd helped her father with its making, she didn't feel like it was her child—this was Wilm's and she had merely been its final midwife. She sensed that everything she and Ide had been through was almost finished; that once she handed over this last thing that they would be able, somehow, to go on more easily. She thought perhaps that the grief might lift from both of them once this was done.

Pol had kept her waiting for twenty minutes and she could feel her temper fraying. *Deep breath, Alix.* She knew nothing would be gained by showing her irritation. Fortunately, she was saved from a further trying of her patience by the opening of the door.

Duke Pol had reached his late thirties without managing to find himself a wife (a distinction he'd shared with his mother). Not for lack of trying—more than one potential bride had met with him and found him not to their taste. He wasn't ill-favoured, but he *was* taciturn and arrogant, and there was an air about him that could best be described as "sullen". However, it was more than that: it felt like suppressed violence, as if any refusal of his desires and wants might be met with the back of a hand or the front of a fist. This day he'd chosen to wear the swan feather cloak his mother had made when he assumed rulership. It was bright white, full-length, and brushed the floor as he walked. Watching him, Alix considered the true nature of swans. Pol took up his seat on the raised dais and his steward, a small man, bald, wizened, followed in his wake like an anxious dog. He fussed with the cloak to ensure it remained as beautiful when the Duke sat. When the little man was satisfied with his efforts, he nodded to Alix.

She approached and knelt before the liege-chair, laying the bundle at the Duke's feet, and gently peeling back the covering. The harp lay shiny and sweet on the purple silk. Pol's eyes widened, and Alix caught that. *Good.*

"I hope, my lord, that you gain much pleasure from this. It was my father's last work, an historic piece as such."

"Well, I have waited long enough for it, so it had better be something special," sneered the Duke.

Alix did not answer. She lifted the harp and strummed a few notes.

In truth, she was barely more than workmanlike with the thing—Ide had the true talent for playing—yet the magic in its creation ensured she sounded like a master. The strings made the room echo with their beauty, and Pol's eyes sparked again. Alix did not let it go, though his hands reached instinctively. Realising what she wanted, he *tsked* in annoyance and jerked his head at the steward. The man fished a purse of gold from somewhere in his robe and held it out to Alix. She pocketed it before handing the instrument to the Duke.

He held the thing like a child and Alix couldn't help but think it an unhappy child at that. Awkwardly he touched the strings; they wailed. *Appropriate*. She kept her eyes cast down.

"My lord, my sister will attend tomorrow for your lessons. I'm sure you will soon be a maestro."

He shook his head, but meant *Yes*, then waved a hand at her: *Begone*. He was fascinated by the harp already, couldn't wait to have it to himself. Alix wondered how much of a temper he'd be in when Ide came to the castle. Would he have smashed the thing by then in a mood? She gave the slightest of curtseys and left.

꙳

Alix knew that Ide's days passed into years, tidying the cottage, cooking for her family, attending to all the domestic chores a mother would otherwise have made her own. She wove and embroidered, sitting with the other women beside the fountain—the old silk-spinners who knew everything that went on—chatting and gossiping while Alix served her apprenticeship with their father.

There was always a hot meal on the table in the evenings and clean sheets on the beds, fresh flowers in the vases and water for washing pulled from the well. Ide gave the cottage its heart, for which Alix was glad because she herself had no domestic inclination.

But that next morning she took her sister's place as little mother

THE BONE LANTERN

and made her porridge with cream, ensured her dress and apron were neat, her hair carefully braided into a coronet around her head, said not a cross word about the skerrick of makeup that rouged Ide's cheeks and lips. Alix handed over Ide's own harp—which she herself had polished and tuned the night before—and sent her on her way with another word of warning about the Swan Prince's temper and a kiss to her cheek. She watched her sister walk quickly along the path that led upwards. There seemed to be a spring in Ide's step and Alix wondered for the first time whether her sister sometimes yearned as she did for a different life; they were twins after all. Different in many ways, but perhaps at their shared heart there was a whim and a wish that might lead them away from this town one day. Perhaps to the ocean to see what their mother had known. Perhaps they would discuss it that night.

Then the thought was gone from her head as Alix began to prepare for her own day.

*

Yet when she returned to the cottage that afternoon, Alix was surprised to find it empty and dark, the hearth cold, no sign of a meal prepared or in the process of being so. She'd expected Ide to spend only a few hours at the castle—that the Duke's limited patience would hardly have allowed for more. Perhaps she was wrong, perhaps she'd been unfair to him; perhaps his love of music had stood him in good stead and gifted him more determination than expected.

She continued to think that for the next hour as she made mushroom soup—not as good as Ide's but edible. She would toast the stale bread; slathering it with butter to cover many sins. Still Ide did not return, and Alix thought perhaps her sister had been caught up with friends, had forgotten about her—but she knew that Ide would never forget her family, not the way Alix sometimes did (or wished she could). She knocked on doors for another hour, first their neighbours and friends, then further out, folk she either knew only by sight, or not at all. By the time she reached Anese's cottage, she was desperate: it was the last place to look, the last but one.

"Have you seen her?" she rushed when the old woman finally came to the door, dressed in her nightgown, hair awry, blinking the fuddle of sleep from her eyes.

"Who?"

"Ide! Who else would I seek?"

"No, not in a day or two, Alix. What's wrong?"

"She's not home. She taught the Duke his first music lessons today, she is not home."

"Her friends?"

"None have seen her."

"The castle, then. Go. I shall search here."

Alix ran up the path in the darkness. She'd never moved so quickly. She fell more than once, skinned hands and knees, chin. At the gates—which stood open because why close them?—four men-at-arms dozed, three against walls, one curled in a corner. She thought they might have roused as she passed, but did not pause to check. She must have looked quite mad and did not want to give anyone an excuse to stop her.

She found her way to the reception hall, which was in darkness but for a few candles. Alix spun and spun, looking for her sister, but seeing only the starry sky of the ceiling. She began to shout Ide's name, louder and louder until her throat was hoarse but the only one she summoned was the steward: bleary-eyed, haunted-looking as an owl, his dressing gown not properly tied. She grabbed him by the front of his robe, hauled him up to face her and shouted.

"Where is my sister?"

"She left hours ago," he stammered.

She felt her rage wash away, gave him a shake, then dropped him. "But where is she?"

"I, I don't know, Alix. She spent a few hours with the Duke, the lessons went well, and then Ide left." He adjusted his night attire and his dignity. "Perhaps she is with a friend?"

She shook her head. "Where is Pol?"

"The Duke is sleeping, as *was* everyone in this castle." His tone was reproachful.

Alix stared at him. He seemed genuine, truthful. He believed what he was saying. Suddenly the energy and rage left her, replaced by the certainty that she would get nothing further from him, that she would soon be dragged out by the men-at-arms who were peeking around the doorframe, awaiting orders.

"I'm sure she will be found quite safe, Alix." The steward touched her arm gently. "I will send these men with you to aid in the search."

She thanked him and wearily began to leave, then paused. "Tell the Duke…"

She hesitated so long he said, "Tell him?"

Alix shook her head, shrugged and turned away.

When she reached the town once again, four guards in tow, it wasn't long before she came to her own cottage and found a crowd outside. The hushed whispering stopped. The sea of folk parted so she could take the few steps up to the open front door.

Someone had laid Ide out on the wooden kitchen table, her pretty dress covered in dirt and dark stains, her body all strange angles despite their efforts. Alix saw where Anese and the two other women whose names she could not remember at that very moment had been picking fragments of grass and twig, berry and leaf from her sister's form. Someone had closed her eyes, but her head rolled to the side, the slant of her neck unnatural, too loose. Ide's right hand was clenched in a grip so tight that death had not broken it, but when Alix approached and touched the small bruised and broken fingers, they fell open like a flower to show a white swan's feather.

It was more than a week before Alix could bring herself to begin.

Anese had not left her side since that terrible night, had made sure she ate something, drank something. In the evening she gave Alix a draft so she slept without dreams for a while at least; the feather she'd found in Ide's palm clutched in her own. The old woman spoke to her in the waking hours, about the things she might do now there was nothing to hold her in this place, and Alix learned that the rumours of the old woman being a witch were more than mere gossip.

The god-hound who'd conducted her father's funeral not so very long ago had knocked at the door every day, trying to convince her that Ide must be buried. Anese advised her to follow the forms, and finally, she consented. Alix sat the vigil beside her sister in the cold, bare church at the edge of the graveyard, said nary a word until the morning, when she whispered, "I'm sorry". It could have been for multiple perceived sins—not even Alix could have articulated what they all were—except for what she was about to do.

Ide was buried in the morning, in the plot that held both their parents. Ide would not long lie beneath, yet Alix had to let those around her think otherwise. She accepted condolences during the wake, managed a nod here and there, and left Anese to answer questions.

When night fell, when lanterns were extinguished and the town slept, Alix went once more to the churchyard, found the shovel the sexton had used to fill in the grave not so many hours ago. Found it, used it, dug deeply into the earth, sweating in the cool black air, until the metal of the blade clunked against the small coffin. It hardly took any effort at all to pry the lid off and lift her sister out—Ide was so small and light after all, and swaddled tight in her shroud to keep the shattered bones in place—then replace the lid, reposition the coffin, fill the hole in once more, to ensure nothing would appear to have been disturbed when the new day dawned.

She carried Ide to the workshop and laid her out on a bench. Alix stared at her sister awhile—her conversation with Old Anese replaying in her head, all those terrible things she needed to do—then at last she got to work. She cut away the green gown her sister had been buried in—no point in saving it, Ide would have no further need. The scraps and shreds dropped to the floor and Alix kicked them aside bit by bit.

All the knives were lined up—she'd sharpened them till they sang—and one of the glass tanks had been emptied and filled again with a special formula. She injected the mixture into Ide's heart to make the coagulated blood fluid once again and siphoned it into a large jar, then blade in hand, she stripped skin and muscle, flesh and tendon from her sister's body. All the meat that had once been Ide slopped and slipped and dripped into copper buckets.

When all the small bones of her twin had been liberated—so many fragments that she would need to reconstruct—she gently slid them into the tank she'd filled with a new liquid, one that Anese had helped her mix. She was careful not to let anything splash her skin or clothes. The bones needed to soak for 12 hours, then be removed to a wash of rainwater for another two days to ensure the corrosive liquid was gone. And the bones would be, for a brief while, as malleable as the wood she'd used to make harps.

※

For a while, the people around her simply took it for grief.

All the many days when she moved only between the house and the workshop, and eventually not even leaving that. The wives left food on the doorstep, and sometimes she took it inside. Sometimes she even ate it. Old Anese kept them at bay, sitting outside so no do-gooder might interrupt—and folk were scared enough of the beldam to listen to her even though their urges said otherwise. *Bring the girl out. Insist she eat and sleep and bathe. Take her to the church, let the god-hound apply a balm to her soul. Arrange the young men in order of attractiveness so she might select a husband from them. She would have children and soon forget her losses.*

"Leave her alone or I'll tear your skin off and turn it into a hat," Old Anese would growl, and none dared test her resolve. They came no closer than the low fence, which was for the best, so no one heard the sounds of incantations being sung, of low weeping, of voices other than Alix's conversing in tones both measured and otherwise.

After four weeks, Alix at last emerged, blinking in the sunlight, smelling so appallingly bad that none would go near her after the Widow Aintree first made that mistake. There were stains on her face and fingers, her clothes clearly having not been changed all that time, and her hair a mess of knots and whorls such that even birds would be unlikely to nest there. Her apron appeared to have been burned in places, and the skin of her wrists, the palms of her hands, the lengths of her forearms all bore the marks of a blade, as if she'd been bled more than once. And she had, for the making of what she held in her arms required almost as much of her as she'd taken from her sister's corpse.

The thing was clearly an instrument but there was something wrong with it. Nothing like the rosewood dital harps she'd spent her life making, nothing like those lovely things with their golden bridges and frets, their nacre inlays, the glow of many coats of resin burnished to a high sheen. Nothing like the elegant shape of those things, and yet...strangely elegant, strangely recognisable.

It was a mixed thing, a harp of bone. Bones bent and reshaped, curved and twisted into a U, but recognisable despite it all. The strings were made from hair as fine and strong as silk, black as ebony, and held in place by fingerbones as white as snow to tighten and tune the thing. And it shone, polished and varnished, the bones darkened

THE BONE LANTERN

under their treatment at Alix's hands, so they might have looked like rubies had their true shape not remained evident.

Even Old Anese, whose knowledge had birthed this idea, was as horrified as she was fascinated. But still, she herded the girl through the gathering folk, back to her cottage. She made Alix wash, eat, and sleep. She pulled the tangles from her hair and braided it neatly. She put out a clean dress and fresh shoes so Alix might look presentable when she next went to visit the Duke.

※

The guardsmen would not have let her in. Alix had seen it in their expressions, uncertainty but also resolution. She thought that the Duke had given orders and felt there could only be one reason for that.

So, she smiled to disarm them, then began to strum the harp—she'd not tried it before lest it affect someone she did not mean to enchant, but the guards would provide a fine test. The notes were beautiful, dark, rang in the cool autumn air so clearly she could almost see them, and sang the word *Stop*. Immediately, the men froze in their tracks, eyes glazed over. Alix had no idea how long the effect might last, so she continued to play as she passed them by, to wander the corridors of the castle.

Wherever she went, she would sing her command over the top of the harp's tune and servants ceased what they were doing. The steward and the Duke's mother came out of a parlour to see the source of the music, but as soon as they heard it clearly, they went the way of the servitors. Alix felt a prick of spite as she paused in front of the two—one had birthed the Duke, the other she was certain had lied for him. The urge to deal with them both almost overthrew her, the rage like an inferno in her mind. But she resisted. After all, she could always come back for them if the desire did not subside.

She found the Swan Prince in his reception hall. Alix's fingers continued to play, she sang *Stop* one last time. He sat in the liege-chair, as immobile as the others in his castle. Only his eyes moved, and the feathers of the swan cloak draped around his shoulders shifted in the breeze that blew through the room.

"I can only imagine that your temper got the better of you," she said sweetly. Alix had given the event considerable thought in the past weeks. "So frustrating to want so badly to play so beautifully, then to find you're simply not able." She shook her head. "Ide was sweet and patient—more so than anyone I've ever known. She'd not have lost her temper with you. Yet even an enchanted instrument could not make your efforts palatable."

His eyes flickered back and forth, almost like the beating of desperate wings. But she saw no denial there, only fear; her mouth watered. Alix moved to the bank of windows, to the spot where a pane of glass was entirely missing.

"It will take such a long while to replace, yes? Waiting for the right materials to arrive, for someone to blow the glass, to engrave it, to remake it as it was. Such a cold breeze all these weeks—will they have it done before full winter, do you think? I didn't notice that night, I was too panicked. But the room was very cold and I should have paused, should have looked more carefully." She stared at him, her fingers moving gently over the strings. "Come here."

And he did though his gait was most unwilling; he resisted with every step. At last, however, he was by her side. "How long before you threw her from the window?"

He simply stared, unable to speak; she decided she did not really care to know. "You'd hurt me too, wouldn't you? If you could. If I set you free."

He blinks once: *Yes.*

"Well, my lord, I'll give you your freedom: jump."

She gazed at him—he fought so hard, an internal struggle etched on his face, his body. Tried so hard to not throw himself from the window. Yet, not hard enough; just to be certain, she strummed once more and repeated, "Jump."

Alix watched him climb onto the thin sill then leap into the void, into the air over the valley. The swan cloak fluttered around him, somehow coming apart as he tumbled, the feathers rising and he falling. No scream escaped his lips.

There was some satisfaction, she thought, but it did not fill the hole left by Ide's death. Perhaps if she sent his mother and steward after him?

Part of her mind and heart had been burned away, she was certain, by the making of that strange harp; surely it wasn't simply the grief of losing her sister. She'd done something terrible—glorious, but terrible—and there had to be cost. She thought it might be part of her humanity. Part of her soul. Who knew? Perhaps she might live forever now, with that weakness gone.

Alix watched until he could no longer be seen, had disappeared into the treetops of the forest below. They'd find him, if they looked, where Ide's body had been discovered. If someone cared to look.

She took the path downward, to the road where Old Anese waited with two horses. Their time in the town was done, and Alix could not imagine that anyone would bother to follow them. She did not know where they would go.

Perhaps towards the sea.

❧

Selke stretches, rolls her shoulders.

The man's eyes are wide, his mouth hangs open with anticipation. He does not ask, though she knows what he's wondering. Once again, she steps inside the small wagon. There is no hesitation, no sound of searching for she knows very well where *this* thing is.

She sits back down, the dital harp in her lap. It gleams blood-red in the light of the fire, the finger bones are now yellowed with age. Her hands on it are tender.

"Where are the strings?" he asks, sounding a little relieved.

Selke shrugs. "I've never found them. Perhaps they did not last as long as the harp. Perhaps their owner took them with her when she left it behind. I think perhaps it was not the worst thing in the world, for them to be lost. Imagine the damage one could do."

"Did she do damage? Alix?"

She nods. "I believe she did."

"Did she find the sea?"

"I believe she did."

"Why do you have it? And the bird?"

"I have found that the best bargains, the ones that cost you the most, are sealed with strange things. I collect such things because I might be able to use them, to negotiate for that which I truly desire."

"Which is?" He leans forward, rapt.

She hesitates, then figures *Why not? What harm? One of them will be gone by dawn.* "A bone lantern."

"What's that?"

"Something to light the way." She feels infinitely ancient, all her secrets weighing her down. "When one gets as old as I, when one has cheated death so many times—and I have done that over and over—an ordinary *decease* will no longer come for one."

He lifts a brow.

"Death simply doesn't want me anymore. So now I must seek it out." She laughs. "Yet there is hope, or so I'm led to believe. In my researches I have read that Lady Death herself keeps a cessation for one such as myself. That I must beg it of her."

"Death is all around," he says.

"But not mine. Not any longer. I did not wait for it, so it now waits for me. I must find the place where it lies, *my* ending. A bone lantern will show my path. I'm so very tired."

They are silent for a while. There is only the crackle of the fire, the creep in the undergrowth of night animals trying not to attract attention. Finally, he says, "I'll come along."

Selke startles—this was not something she'd expected. "Why?"

"Doesn't every deathless creature seek peace one day?"

She wonders again how long he's roamed the earth, how long he's been as he is, what he did to deserve it. But before she can ask, there is a flare of fiery orange through the trees.

Dawn comes fast in this part of the world. The light washes over both of them and for a moment Selke is blinded. When she at last blinks her sight back, she sees the stone wolf. He's changed to his four-legged self, and the sunrise has petrified him; the result she'd hoped for while she distracted him with stories. Now it's happened, it's irksome. Hard to get answers from a rock.

Selke sits for a while, considering.

She's still curious—she's weary, not dead, and her mind will poke and prod at the conundrum of him until she can no longer think straight—she might break off a piece of his tail, examine it, experiment on it, see what she can find out and document. She might pack up her wagon, quickly-quickly, and put as much distance as she can between herself and the creature; but she suspects he'd sniff out her trail no matter where or how far she went.

Selke picks up the apple she's neglected throughout her tale-telling; she's hungry and he's eaten all the rabbit. She settles back to wait.

Author's Note

Readers of other stories set in my *Sourdough* world will recognise Selke. She first appeared in "A Porcelain Soul" in *Sourdough and Other Stories*. She pops up again in the novella *Of Sorrow and Such*. And again in "Sleeping Like Snow" in *The Tallow-Wife and Other Tales*.

"The Bone Lantern" gave me a chance to revisit Selke a few months after the events of The Tallow-Wife, but also to reach back into the past of this world, to a time before the other tales are set. In them you might recognise characters from "The Promise of Saints" and the novel *All the Murmuring Bones*.

Thanks to Marie O'Regan for asking: "So, you got anything for Absinthe?" (or words to that effect, more pleasantly phrased), to PS Publishing for kindly thinking my stories are worth taking, and to Ron Serdiuk, as ever, for his excellent critical eye on early drafts.